Forever Awaiting Redemption

by

Declan James

DORRANCE PUBLISHING CO
EST. 1920
PITTSBURGH, PENNSYLVANIA 15238

This is a work of fiction. Names, characters, places, and incidents are either the product of the author's imagination or are used fictitiously, and any resemblance to actual persons, living or dead; events; or locales is entirely coincidental.

Dorrance Publishing Co
585 Alpha Drive
Suite 103
Pittsburgh, PA 15238
Visit our website at *www.dorrancebookstore.com*

ISBN: 979-8-89211-037-2
eISBN: 979-8-89211-535-3

To The Readers, The Ones Who Know That Things Are Never What They Seem And Study Their Surroundings To Connect The Dots

"Sometimes, being different feels a lot like being alone. But with that being said, being true to that and being true to my standards and my way of doing things in my art and music, everything that has made me feel different…in the end, it has made me the happiest."

~ Lindsey Sterling

Six Months Ago

The crackle of the flames in the river-stone hearth and the occasional rustle of black-feathered wings, as my brothers shifted in their chairs and or on their plush colourful cushions, were the only reminders to me that I hadn't fallen unconscious in the warm, dim room. The wind howled and whistled as it found its way through the cracks of the mansion's infrastructure, but at least the snow wasn't getting inside. Amongst each other in hushed whispers, which was difficult considering how rough their voices were, Anam and Fergal were murmuring to one another about a mistake the other had made during a rather messy game of poker. Fergal thumbed through the cards, a rather difficult thing to do seeing as he didn't have a thumb and had to sort them with his pointer finger. Occasionally I heard the others debating about when Bowen would return home from his "outing," even though we all knew that's not what it was, and had such more malevolent intention than such an innocent word conveyed. Boyd had his big, freckled nose buried in a book, so soaked in coffee and tea stains that I couldn't tell if the book's cover had ever originally been white. It was titled *Good Omens*, written by two *human* authors, a rather peculiar occurrence here, with a cross-legged demon on the cover, looking suave in his sunglasses and suit. Boyd's green eyes glinted in the dull fire light as his eyes darted back and forth across the musty pages that crackled every time he turned them. I cracked my knuckles and tapped my fingers impatiently on the side table and waited anxiously, taking a sip of water every few minutes to keep my hands busy as I listened to the old grandfather clock, Cathal's sword and Caelan's prized violin propped up against the mahogany. *Tick Tock.* A second went by, and then there it was again, the incessant ticking, the only thing marking the passage of time. *Tick Tock, Tick Tock, Tick Tock.* Then there it was, the creak of rusted and unoiled door hinges interrupted my train of useless thought and announced the arrival we'd been anticipating and dreading. Bowen, soaking wet and stumbling, treading mud and slush into the room and on the antique carpet, almost drunkenly careless. But Bowen didn't drink. That was out of the question; he hated the bitter taste of the alcohol on his tongue and blatantly refused to indulge with the rest of us. At least not since Caelan's birth as far as we knew.

"Boas noites," he said, as he flopped onto the embroidered sofa and crossed his legs.

"Boas noites," many of the others mumbled in response, as he got comfortable and sank into the cushions, for the broken springs offered no support for his weight, despite his petite frame. He shifted positions and draped his arm over the edge of the sofa as if attempting to showcase the half-dried blood on his forearm. The dark red, nearly black liquid was a stark contrast to his pale skin and had even stained the cuff of his torn shirt sleeve. It was still sticky and seemed as if it had oozed from Bowen's own skin, but we all knew it hadn't. Caelan stared at Bowen in pure and utter shock with a slight hint of fear playing across his face, his bright blue eyes widening in complete and utter, innocent curiosity.

"Is he…?" Caelan inquired timidly. Bowen nodded and smiled with satisfaction. "Oh my," the 12-year-old whispered in a hushed tone of concern.

"About time, right?" Bowen laughed coldly, the light from the fire illuminating his scar that covers the right side of his face. A cruel smile on his face. His lips drawing back over his teeth to reveal pearly white teeth behind them.

"Is that...?" the child implored, gesturing to the blood on Bowen's arm. "Is it his?" Bowen raised his eyebrow.

"Whose else's would it be, you little bastard?" Caelan looked down at their book and didn't say anything else.

"Sorry, Bowen."

"Lorcan?" Bowen hissed, ignoring Caelan. "A word?" He leapt up lithely from the sofa and jerked his head in the direction of the side room door.

"I'm coming." I pushed up my glasses and got up, Caelan's curious eyes followed me all the way to the side room door, and I mouthed, *You okay?* As I edged past them, they looked away from me as if trying to hide behind their red bangs, not acknowledging my concern for their wellbeing. Bowen was holding the door open for me and the moment I was inside he closed and locked the door, even though I didn't see him do it, but I could hear the rapid series of clicks and snaps and that was enough for me to know that I was trapped. The smell of mouse feces and rotting food was an overpowering stench that could've been compared to the Lagoon on the other side of Faelan near the marshlands. I gagged.

"What was that?" Bowen asked.

"Nothing," I answered, attempting to hide my grimace. The candles illuminated the room, and the menacing chains hanging on walls near unoccupied torch brackets. Bowen had his back to me, his eyes, even though I couldn't see them, were fixated on the wall I couldn't see.

"We need to talk." Bowen whipped around and cuffed me to the wall, the manacles tightened, and the sharp edges dug into my wrists, reopening old wounds from the week prior.

"Que carallo, Bowen!" I screeched as my wings were flattened completely to my back and almost felt as if they were being pinched.

"Language," Bowen hissed, looking up at me. "There are children in the next room over, remember?"

"Bastard," I murmured under my breath. I started squirming in the chains attempting to shake them off, but they only got tighter.

"Yes?" Bowen replied sarcastically, grinning at me through the gloom. "What is it?"

"Parafuso, you know that's not what I meant." He shrugged smugly, and I knew he was about to say something he found witty.

"Maybe I did, maybe I didn't. You tell me." With a flick of his wrist the cuffs vanished and there were red burn marks where they once been that made it look as if I had had hot metal brand bands on my forearms and the slash wounds from the dagger I kept in my bedside table were reopened and bleeding fresh blood.

"Overkill, don't you think?" Bowen arched an eyebrow and cocked his head to the side.

"No, I don't believe so, what makes you say that?" He smirked and his eyes darted to my wrists and then back up to my face.

"What did you need to talk about, smartass?"

"What occurred this evening. By the cliff." I felt a twinge of guilt as he said those words, but it was nothing compared to the sickening fear that had settled in the pit of my stomach. Remembering what I had done, leaving him alone there to fend for himself against the most powerful deity on the island and our father.

"I know, I froze, it won't happen again." Bowen's eyes turned to green flames. Flames that would scorch anyone who got to close.

"You sure as hell won't." His arm snaked around my throat, and he pulled me close, his wings spread in what I presumed was meant to be a highly intimidating stance and hissed into my ear and an icy sharp piece of blood-stained metal dug into my skin. I felt a warm liquid trickle down the side of my neck and felt Bowen's cool breath caress my ear, but his words were rougher than his demeanour. "If you mess up again," he dug the dagger deeper into my neck, "it'll be your life on the line."

"Let me go you sick nai de puta pequena," I hissed. Bowen loosened his grip and stared me in the eye.

"Would you kill Caelan for me?"

"*Our* Caelan?" He nodded. "The child in the next room over?" He nodded again.

"Who else?"

"But why?"

"Does the name Lilith ring a bell? One parent was gone, now the other is. Now let's just end the memory of them both, the memories die with the youngest who never had them." Bowen's entire demeanour changed as he said our mother's name. He let go of me, and I placed my hand on his shoulder, almost in a comforting way but keeping him at a safe distance simultaneously.

"Bowen, it wasn't their fault, they were a baby."

"But he was the last of Isan's heirs. The last potential Oheria heir to rule Faelan. It must have been a sign from the gods she died giving birth to them. How is it not their fault?" I sighed.

"They were an infant who was not responsible for their actions." A tear rolled down Bowen's cheek.

"It should've been them, not her."

"I agree." Bowen's eyes narrowed, and he looked crazed. He yanked me forward by the collar and looked into my eyes. I could almost feel heat coming from the green flames that were boring into my soul.

"Then you'll help me?" He looked feral and deranged. "You'll help me kill them?" I couldn't kill a child, but maybe I could find a way around ending their life without Bowen ever finding out, but that was an issue for future Lorcan.

"I'll assist you," I announced.

"Good, marvellous," Bowen said, almost as if he was speaking to himself. "Absolutely lovely, you're free to leave." As I made my way to the door Bowen spoke again. "Oh, and one other thing." He turned around and stared into my eyes. "Don't go to that Skin-Walker for help, not even he could prevent your fate if I found out you went behind my back. If I find out you two are still in contact, it won't end well for either of you." We both knew that Balarin had a genetic defect, making it impossible to change form or maybe it was too painful, but his magic wouldn't be much against Bowen's blade and we both knew it, he may be manipulative but he couldn't talk his way out of everything. I nodded and as I walked out of the dungeon-like room I felt the fear and panic begin to sink in, but not for me. For the young 12-year-old child who hadn't asked for any of this and would suffer in my place. The same child who had been unknowingly sentenced to death in my place. The innocent child who had never met their mother, whom their father had never loved. The expendable extra. Caelan wouldn't die, but I would make sure that somehow and some-day, hopefully someday soon, it would be Bowen who would be gone.

~The Oheria Legacy~

12 Years Ago

The screams were something I'd never forget, high and scared. The shouting upstairs and the new baby crying, the overwhelming sounds overlapping each other, arguing, crying, screaming. Anger, flat out rage, remorse. I paced around in circles at the bottom of the stairs. Biting my nails anxiously as I waited for someone to come down and update me. It was just me and my thoughts as Aman, Fergal, and Boyd were already tucked in bed. Once you were past 10 years of age there were no rules; being 11 and Bowen 12, we were exceptions to the Oheria heir curfew.

"Can you shut that thing up!?" Isan's loud, gruff voice was hard to misplace amongst the various shouts from Seraphim Landry. I shuddered at the sound of hostility in my father's tone. Then everything was quiet except for the crying infant that was likely scared and confused. Bowen came rushing down the stairs, his hands clamped tightly over his ears blocking the noise, his face stained with tears and crimson liquid.

"What happened?" I asked, rushing to him and wrapping my arm around his shoulders. His feathers were dishevelled, and there was a bloody slash on his cheek, source of the red. "Are you alright?"

"Do I look alright!?" he screeched, pushing me away and storming off to the stairwell.

"I demand you tell me what happened," I demanded, sprinting in front of him to block the way to the stairs that led to the wing where our rooms were.

"Get out of the way," he hissed. "Don't make me push you."

"Where's Mum? Where's the baby?" I asked.

"The baby's fine, Father named it Caelan," he said, shoving me out of the way. I didn't think he'd actually do it.

"And Mum?" I asked, my stomach doing somersaults with anxiety. "Mr. Landry's here, or was, I haven't seen him come back downstairs,"

"Bugger off," Bowen grumbled, attempting to slam his door, but I stopped it with my foot.

"Maybe I just didn't see him," I condoned, "but he's only summoned if something's wrong." Bowen stared out his window, using his shirt sleeve to wipe the blood off his cheek, not answering me right away.

"She's gone." Bowen sobbed. Falling face first onto his pillow and began uncontrollably shaking. My heart sank. Mum was only 28. She had had Bowen at 16, me at 17, Anam and Fergal were twins, and she had them at 21. Boyd was born two years and now Caelan. She was too young to die; she was barely a child herself, and she hadn't lived for herself yet. All she had really done in life was take care of us and even though she said she was happy, I could hear her and Father screaming at one another, and I knew she was lying. But now she was gone. Mother hadn't asked for this or us. The Oheria Legacy was a Legacy forged in tradition and bloodlust, and Lilith had been claimed by that lust for power and continuation of the bloodline. In a family like ours, redemption wasn't something the gods would ever give us. People thought we were a Legacy forged in redemption, but the locals of Faelan were so deeply misled and convinced that I began to believe the lies myself.

"Hmm?" I asked, snapping out of my thought, realising that Bowen had been speaking.

"I'm going to kill that man," he repeated. "It's *his* fault that any of this even happened in the first place." Bowen sat up, wiping his tears and blood on his shirt sleeve.

"Who?" I asked. "There's a lot of gentlemen in this manor, you'll need to be more specific."

"Father." I arched an eyebrow and he then chuckled softly to himself at the sight of my expression. "We could do it together?" he suggested. Bowen shrugged, standing up and walking over to his nightstand.

"I suppose we could," I replied. Bowen took a small bottle and cloth out of the drawer and doused the rag in the foul-smelling liquid before placing it on his face.

"Do you know what this is?" he asked, sitting down and crossing his legs, one hand on his knee and the other holding the rag to his face.

"Something you shouldn't have?" I guessed, and Bowen laughed, a harsh sound I'd never heard escape his throat before.

"I suppose you could say that," he said. "It's the extract from the processed pulp of Faelinin flowers. Do you know what those are?" he asked. I shook my head. "It's a drug," he said flatly.

"Oh."

"Yeah," he replied. "The flowers ingested whole can kill you, just like any drug in large quantities," he added, applying more of the Faelinin to his face. "But—" he continued. "It helps with pain; the only drawback is that it's addictive. In its unprocessed form you can smoke the petals like human marijuana, not that I expect you know what tha—"

"I do, actually," I interrupted. "Saw it in one of Boyd's textbooks." Bowen rolled his eyes.

"Overachieving bastard," he muttered. He tilted his head to the side, showcasing his new scar. "Is it still bleeding?" he asked. I shook my head.

"It looks fine, it was a rather clean cut." Bowen nodded thoughtfully at this.

"There's that at least." He chuckled. The scent of the Faelinin was pungent and filled my head with a thick haze, making it difficult for coherent thoughts to make it to the forefront of my brain. I wrinkled my nose. "Bad, eh?" He laughed. "I'm not a big fan of the scent, either."

"Well, there is something we have in common," I said, trying not to gag which was easier said than done.

"Y'know," he started, "we're heirs, someday we'll be in charge." I looked up at him.

"I don't want to be an heir," I stated. "I wish I could just go away, get away from it all, bend the rules."

"Admit it, you'd be a good lord."

"I really wouldn't." Bowen shrugged.

"Whatever you say, Lorcan." He got up and stored away the Faelinin and rag. He rummaged through the drawer for a moment, sifting through the random junk until he found what he was looking for. He uncorked the bottle and took a swig before handing it to me. "Want some?" I took the bottle, suspiciously sniffing the contents.

"Why do you have this?" I asked. Bowen shrugged again, as if it was normal to have a bottle of rum stored in your nightstand.

"Why shouldn't I have it?" he answered. "No one else drinks it, do they?" I handed it back to him.

"I'll pass." Bowen took another sip.

"Lightweight." He chuckled.

"I prefer sensible."

"Don't worry, it's my last bottle anyways." He corked it and tucked it under his pillow. I watched him apprehensively. "It helps me sleep," he said, answering my unasked question.

"Is Caelan a boy or a girl?" I asked, changing the subject. Bowen rolled his eyes and laid down on his bed, getting settled in.

"Intersex," he grumbled. "Not really much use for the bloodline, if you ask me."

"Quite a harsh statement to use on an infant who hasn't had a chance to prove its worth, don't you think?" Bowen just glowered up at me drunkenly. "Perhaps they'll marry into a powerful family," I suggested.

"Who cares," Bowen murmured, burrowing into his blankets. "Don't answer that, it was rhetorical."

"I do," I replied, ignoring his request. "And so should you."

"I need time," he said. "I just need to process everything, please leave." I got up and walked over to the door. "It's Caelan's fault." I ignored him, not bothering to ask what he meant and closed the door behind me.

~The Letter to Cummacdh~

Six Months Ago

I walked to my room, closing the door behind me, contemplating the request Bowen had given me. Caelan was a child after all; they didn't deserve to be punished for something they couldn't help, and I had been entrusted with the duty of making sure they didn't make it out of the manor alive. I locked the door, not wanting Bowen to barge in and confront me again before I had made up my mind. He had made it rather clear that it was Caelan or me, but I didn't want to choose. There could be no in between or compromise to be had with him, unless…

I lay down on my bed, wrapping myself in my quilt embroidered with a phoenix Boyd had given me last Fallen Festival, a gift from Melodian the nymph. I looked out the rust-encrusted window, the snow upon the ground whiter than the shells on the beach near the Anamearian Ocean. I shuddered; it was colder than a version of frozen over Hell. But Hell, or at least human Hell, was likely more peaceful than Faelan. Every other day there was a new story about Isan's reign of terror across the small island, but not anymore. Bowen had seen to that; I remembered when he had first told me of his intentions two years ago. And I had watched as he had used the same silver-bladed dagger to threaten me this evening, stab our father, gouge his wings out of his skin, and leave the bloody feathers to be blown away by the wind. I shuddered and felt sick to my stomach at the thought of going for a walk on the grounds and accidentally stumbling upon one of the feathers. Gods knew what that would trigger in my head. I don't believe I could ever walk past that cliff again. I saw Isan's blood stain the pure snow and saw Bowen's ripped sleeve and tarnished boots from Isan's nails as he had been scrabbling to hold on before falling and crashing into icy, harsh, and brutal waves below. The sound of the whipping wind and the snow were the only things preventing us from hearing his screams. Bowen, deranged, dishevelled, and mad, watched with glee and that's when I ran. Desperate to leave the place, the sight of the blood making me sick.

Now the only thought I could think of was seeing Caelan, instead of Isan's crumpled body at the base of the cliff, or their blood dripping through the floorboards as they begged me for help. *Lorcan, please!* I shuddered, trying to rid the sound of their sweet yet desperate voice from my head, impossible to do. I was there when they cried for the first time, I was there when they walked for the first time. First word, first sentence, first step. I had seen it all, and watching all of that progress end before my eyes was something I knew I couldn't live with. I closed my eyes, hoping I would succumb to sleep, but no. And even if I had it wouldn't have been peaceful; it would be nightmarish and cruel just like my brother and late father before him. I didn't know how Bowen was able to live with himself after hearing Isan's screams. He was a despicable person, but he was still our father. But fate was easily changed, and I was foolish to have not seen it sooner. I sat up and swung my feet over the edge of the bed and the floorboards creaked as I got up and strode over to my desk. I withdrew a pen and piece of paper from the bottom drawer, removed the cap with my teeth, and spit it onto the floor and began hurriedly writing down every little thing that had happened in the past five hours.

My Dearest Friend Balarin,

Balarin knew Isan and my family better than anyone, but they didn't know him, giving us the advantage as potential partners in crime. All the better reason to keep him in the loop but no one else on the island. He would take secrets to the grave. At least those were the rumours.

Sincerely, Your Dearest Acquaintance, Lorcan Isan

Balarin would know exactly what to do, and he was a rather punctual and trustworthy correspondent as I knew from our other various encounters. I dug around in my pocket, withdrawing a pencil and a few marbles. I guess I hadn't just lost them metaphorically, there were three, there were supposed to be four. I kept rummaging until I finally found what I was looking for: a small piece of kitchen string. I rolled up the parchment and tied the string around it. I shook it around by the end of the string to make sure it was tight enough and placed it in a small satchel attached to my belt, which I fastened tightly around my waist. I ran and leapt out of the window, spreading my wings and gliding down to the local apothecary in town. My feet hit the cold solid earth. I folded my wings to my back and bowed my head to avoid smacking into the doorframe as I walked in, my coat swishing and the bell ringing as the door closed behind me.

"Good evening, Young Lord," the shopkeeper said welcomingly and with a smile, not a fake smile, a real one, as she turned around to greet me.

"Good evening, Melodian," I said to the young nymph. "And please, I've said many times," I continued, exasperatedly. *Please,* I begged, "call me Lorcan."

"Alright Lorcan, what can I help you with this lovely evening?" she asked, looking at me sappily. I looked around the small space, contemplating if there was anything I was running out of for my personal storage room, attempting to avoid her piercing blue eyes which were directly fixated on my face, feeling as if they were boring two burning holes into the side of my face, for all I knew maybe she was. I shifted my weight from my left foot to the right and rustled my wings in discomfort. *Please take the hint,* I prayed. *Stop looking at me.* She didn't.

"Umm, err…" I glanced around the apothecary making sure that there wasn't anything missing from my personal list. Send a note to Balarin, get extra ziryan root and a small pack of dried faelinin flowers. "I have to send this note to the Caves of Cummacdh." I withdrew the small scroll and placed it on the counter. "Be discreet with it, will you?" Melodian arched an eyebrow.

"Have a secret correspondence, do you?" she asked, batting her eyelashes at me. She reached for my hand, and I quickly withdrew it from the counter. I was not about to let a nymph touch me. Manipulative through touch, they were known for that.

"It's something I didn't wish my brothers to find out about. You have siblings, surely you understand." She nodded.

"Understandable." She paused before continuing. "But you're not…you know, are you?" She looked hurt.

"Courting? No. I'm not and I have no will to do so any time soon," I lied.

Melodian sighed. "What a pity, you'd be such a good suitor to many a young lass."

"Or young lad," I reminded her, with a wink and a smirk. "Has your brother been around lately?" She scowled.

"Tanyan?" she replied, grudgingly. "No."

"That's the real pity here." She looked away from me scornfully.

"Anything else besides the delivery Lord?" she asked as she grabbed the small scroll of the counter.

"Lorcan. Also a small parcel of ground up ziryan root. Por favour." I paused, looking back to see if there was anything I had missed. "Oh!" I exclaimed. "And a small bag of dried faelinin flowers, almost forgot about those."

"Nai de puta, you're quite the dark horse, aren't you? You know what faelinin flowers can do, right?" she hissed under her breath.

"You are aware that I'm fluent in Galician, aren't you?" Her face turned a brighter shade of red than the twin moons of Faelan. "And yes, I'm aware, *don't* tell anyone I purchased them."

"Merda."

"Please, miss, stop swearing. I beg you." She nodded and began packing my small bag with my items and tying the small knot to an old decrepit phoenix's leg. She picked up the phoenix gently and carried him to the window. Not meeting my gaze the whole while.

"Safe travels, Trono." The crimson bird then with a whoosh of wings and rustle of feathers, and a clap of thunder vanished into the night. Perhaps that was where he got his name. The ancient god of thunder, Trono. But perhaps I'd never know. She turned back to me and handed me my parcel. "That'll be seven colares."

"Many Faelan citizens actually believed that Faeries are the evolved variation of phoenixes."

"I believe I asked to be paid in currency, not trivia, Lord." I rolled my eyes and sighed.

"It's Lorcan," I corrected her, for what felt like the millionth time.

"I don't care." She held out her palm, and I dropped seven small turquoise coins into her palm. "Have a good journey back to the manor," Melodian called as I turned to leave, her eyes full of despair at not getting closer to me. She never would but it was funny to watch her try; I wasn't cruel and didn't want to lead her on.

"I will, thank you, Melodian." I ran outside only to find that the snow had turned to a torrential downpour and the moons made it look as if the sky was raining blood. Perhaps I was imagining it. Or maybe it really was blood falling from the night sky in Faelan that evening. A lord had died and hopefully soon would another, at my hand.

~Malevolent Promises~

Two Years Ago

I darted up the winding stairs and ran into my room, slamming the door behind me. The walls shook, and I was surprised no one came running to investigate. The sting of the slashes from Isan's belt burned on my back near where flesh met feathers. I hadn't yet seen the marks and had no wish to. My fingertips no longer had feeling in them. The flames from the candles had melted the flesh that had once been there and enabled feeling in my fingers, but my nerves were burned. At least I hadn't had a finger removed. Fergal wouldn't likely be doing so well in the morning. I hope Boyd had some spare bandages from the apothecary. I stumbled over to the window, gripping the sill tightly, and my knuckles turned white as I looked out across the grounds and toward the Caves of Cummacdh where Balarin was likely heading. I wondered why he didn't stay in town near his mother, but I never thought to ask as it was none of my business and as for his father… Well, he never mentioned him. There was a knock at the door.

"Come in," I said, my voice a low croak, thick with emotion and suppressed screams and tears. The doorknob turned, and Bowen walked inside to join me beside the balcony, even though I didn't see him right away I knew he was there. The familiar clunk of his black leather boots was hard to misplace.

"You alright?" he inquired. "I heard you had it worse tonight." I shrugged and that simple movement stung.

"Nothing I'm not used to," I responded bitterly. Bowen grabbed my shoulders, his hands rough but I could tell he was trying to be gentle as best he could.

"One of these days I'll do something about him," Bowen promised. "Someday." I looked over at him and his eyes were full of a kind of fury I had never seen there before, turning his green eyes into emerald flames. "May I take a look?" I arched an eyebrow. "I want to see how bad it is, see if Boyd has anything that could help." I shrugged again, fumbling with the buttons on my shirt so Bowen could see the damage and it stung.

"How bad is it?" I asked, not wanting to know. I looked over my shoulder and saw Bowen grimace as he appraised the still oozing wounds.

"I'll be right back," he muttered and exited the room, I heard the pitter-patter of his footsteps going down the stairs and to the dungeons where Boyd kept his hidden stash of supplies he didn't want our father finding. Even 10-year-old Caelan was able to find them, it was a shock that Isan hadn't yet. I strode over to my bed and sat down, folding my shirt and placing it at the foot of my bed. I listened to the gentle hum of the wildlife outside and enjoyed the peacefulness of it all, a break from the pain. A moment of calm in the storm that was only broken by the sound of a fist rapping on glass. I looked up and saw a pair of owlish eyes looking back at me from the dark. I got up and opened the window. Balarin clambered inside rather ungracefully and landed on my bed gasping for air and shivering.

"It so fucking cold." He laughed. "Thanks for letting me in, meu amor."

"What are you doing?" I hissed. "Bowen will be back soon; he can't see you in here." Balarin's eyes softened as he looked at me, and I knew I couldn't stay upset with him for long even if I tried. I flopped onto the bed beside him, and he stroked my feathers as I leaned into him. He touched my shoulder blade and a searing pain shot across my back.

"Ahh!" I yelled. Balarin recoiled, trying to find the source of my pain, his face full of concern.

"What's wrong, meu amor?" he asked, his voice full of worry. "Did I do something wrong?" The door opened, and Bowen sauntered in, his arms full of herbs.

"I heard a scream. What—" He stopped when he saw me in Balarin's arms. "What the fuck." Balarin let go of me in a lightning fast second.

"It's not what it looks like—" Balarin said, attempting to assure Bowen, but he had seen all he needed to draw a conclusion. Bowen dropped the herbs and grabbed Balarin's collar and shoved him against the wall, dagger at his throat, the blade already digging into the skin.

"Who are you?" Bowen hissed. "What did you do to Lorcan?" Balarin struggled against Bowen's firm grip. Balarin was taller but definitely not anywhere near equal in strength to Bowen, who had strengthened himself over the years to resist Isan's wrath.

"I didn't do *anything*." He gasped, desperately clawing at Bowen's hands to try to get him to relinquish the knife. "Just let me go." Bowen pressed the blade harder into Balarin's skin, and bright crimson blood started to trickle from his throat to the collar of his button-down. Balarin screeched, a horrid sound, and bared his teeth at Bowen.

"Bowen, stop!" I commanded. "He didn't do anything." Bowen sighed irritably, and loosened his grip. Balarin gasped, enjoying the feeling of air filling his lungs again. He clamped one hand against his throat, ebbing the flow of blood and stumbled over to my bed flopping down beside me again. His teeth returning to their usual length, the elongation of his canines was a mere defensive last resort.

"You didn't answer my question," Bowen growled, reluctantly putting his dagger back in its sheath. "Who are you?"

"Balarin Landry," Balarin answered, extending his right hand, the left still against his neck. "Son of Elowyn and Seraphim Landry." Bowen reluctantly shook his hand, noting Balarin's demeanour and limp wrist.

"What are you doing in my brother's room?" Bowen hissed.

"I hope I'm not intruding," Balarin said, his voice dripping with politeness and sincerity. "I assure that wasn't my intention. I came to the first place I could find to seek a safe place from the storm." Bowen glared sceptically at Balarin and then at me. I averted my eyes to avoid his piercing and disappointed gaze.

"Are those the herbs from Boyd?" I asked, gesturing to the leaves on the floor in an attempt to diffuse the tension between the three of us. Bowen nodded, not taking his gaze off Balarin. I got up to get them, but Balarin gently pushed me back down onto the bed.

"I'll get them," he said, walking past Bowen and scooping them up. Bowen's hand twitched to his blade as Balarin passed but he didn't go any further than that.

"I'll pretend none of this happened as it seems you're merely here to help. Isan wouldn't be glad to know you were here, Mr. Landry." Balarin nodded in agreement. "I won't be as lenient next time, either, if I see you with my brother again. I know what you're doing."

"I don't expect you to be."

Bowen pivoted on his heel and left the room, leaving nothing but silence in his wake.

"Are you alright?" I asked, eyeing the bloody mark on Balarin's neck. He chuckled.

"I should be asking you that, don't worry about me." I looked at the floor as Balarin ground the herbs in a small bowl, which he mixed with water and began applying the mixture to the wounds around my wings.

"What happened?" Balarin asked, gently rubbing the liquid into the wounds in circular motions on my skin. "It's rarely this bad."

"Isan wasn't pleased that I was outside. Don't worry, he didn't see you." I sighed. "I'm surprised Bowen took you being here so well, ow," I whimpered. Balarin flinched away from the sound.

"He won't be next time," Balarin said, his voice full of remorse. "You heard what he said."

"Perhaps he'll get used to you."

"I highly doubt it."

"He's not as terrible as he seems, love."

"That's how it always starts," Balarin's voice lowered, and I could see something in his eyes that had never been there before. "I should know, Seraphim." I arched my eyebrow. "My father," Balarin said, his voice raspy, "he wasn't the most supportive person in Faelan, that's for sure, and I doubt Bowen will be any different." Balarin's voice was thick with sorrow and hopelessness as he spoke, and I gently cupped his face with my hands after he'd finished tending to my scars.

"What did Bowen mean when he said he knew what you were doing?"

Balarin stood up and walked to the window. "He thinks I'm using you. He thinks you're gullible, and I'm using it to my advantage to gain status."

"But you wouldn't do that."

"Exactly," he muttered. "I have no reason too, you're the only one for me." Brushing his lips against my forehead, "Take care, meu amor." And then he was gone.

"You as well," I whispered, but he was already out of sight.

~The Accomplice~

Six Months Ago

The *click, click, click,* of my black heeled boots going up the spiralling stone stairs reverberated harshly off the walls of the 100-year-old cobblestone and would not likely be able to hold up within the next decade or so and would need to be replaced. I'd have to make note of that. Breahninn was rather fond of renovations and would likely enjoy an opportunity of utilising his knowledge of construction and engineering. He *loved* showing off. I walked into my room and closed the door quietly behind me, not wanting to disturb anyone in the manor and alert anyone to the fact that I had been out and about past curfew. There would be a fire storm in the local news outlets tomorrow once everyone found out about Isan's "disappearance." I wonder what Bowen's excuse would be. Drunk and fell over the edge of the cliff? Picked off by Balarin? Somehow. Balarin wouldn't dare so that wouldn't even be an option. For those who knew him were aware he wasn't capable of such blasphemous things such as murder. He would love to be an accomplice to such things but wouldn't dare do anything that would get blood on his expensive, nearly 10,000 colare cloak.

Rushing to the wardrobe I riffled through one of the drawers and began stuffing my parcels in them near my socks and boxers. Bowen wouldn't dare look there unless he wanted a good right hook to the jaw. He knew I could punch, and hard. We had learned this lovely little fact when I was 11 when Bowen had stolen my flute. Mother had given him a rather stern talking to after the fact, however. I walked to the bed and began folding up my embroidered cloak to put away into the closet for my next excursion to town, and who knew when that would be.

"Good evening, Lorcan," a calm, silky voice whispered in my ear. The coolness of the voice paralysed my entire body and stopped my heart for a fraction of a second before I regained my ability to move and breathe again.

"*Eek!*" I gasped, tripping and falling back onto the bed. The pillows significantly cushioning my fall. "¡Fillo de puta!" I screeched. "Couldn't you have given me a warning, could you?" I asked, breathlessly.

"Why would I do that, Lorcan? It's not nearly as funny to watch." Balarin chuckled. His dramatic eyeliner only emphasising the shape of his beautiful, owlishly orange eyes that were glinting in the dimly lit room. The scar on his neck made a vivid contrast to his dark skin. He leaned forward, placing a hand on either side of me. I swallowed and my eyes unfocused. Not sure where to look. "How are you after the, err, encounter with Bowen in the sidero—"

"How did you get here so quickly?" I interrupted, still not focused, my eyes looking *anywhere* other than his face.

"I have my ways, Lorcan." He winked, lifting a hand to stroke my feathers, then his face became serious again. "Please answer my question, I was gravely worried when I received your letter."

"Anxious, worried, nervous—" I sighed, and felt the panic begin to rise and all I could think about was the fact that Balarin was here with me right now. Here because I needed him, and only inches away from me. I wrapped my arms around his neck and locked my mouth to his. He collapsed, falling onto my bed before hurriedly propping himself up with his arms again.

"Is that the real reason you asked me to come over?" He chuckled. "A snog?"

"Perhaps that was part of it." Balarin grabbed my chin, tilted my head up, stared into my eyes, the cold band of his family ring touching my skin, but I ignored its iciness. His gaze softened, and his irises looked like the most gorgeous shade of caramel I'd ever seen. He fixed his mouth to mine. The pitter-patter of the rain and the sound of our breathing was the only noise in the room. His lips were soft and kissable, and I found myself never wanting this feeling to end. I had made it evident that I wasn't going to be the one to end the kiss. I wrapped my arms around his waist and held him there. I didn't want to let go but I did when Balarin made it obvious that he'd had enough and pulled his face away from mine.

"Still anxious?" Balarin asked. "Or would you like me to kiss you again?" I gasped, trying to catch my breath.

"No," I responded, still recovering. "Any plans for the Fallen Festival?" I asked.

"It's six months away." He laughed.

"Never too early to ask," I pointed out, wondering if he would pick up on my not-so-subtle implication.

"I'll be there, don't worry, you can have my first dance." Balarin looked over my shoulder at the drawers where I had hid my parcel. "Off topic, but what did you put in there?" he asked, looking at the drawer and then looking at me again, his voice dripping with curiosity.

"I think you already know," I responded, still adjusting myself and attempting to re-regulate my breathing.

"I don't actually," he said, calmly.

"Really?" I asked, sceptically. "Are you lying to me?"

"No, I may be manipulative but I'm not a very good liar and when I do lie, I speak half-truths. You've been telling me to stay out of your head and respect your privacy," he continued. "That's what I've been doing." His orange eyes warmed. "I've been respecting your boundaries, isn't that what you wanted?" I nodded.

"Yes, of course, I'm just surprised you listened to me. You rarely do." Balarin chuckled, his eyes glittering with amusement.

"Could you please answer my question?" my Balarin whispered. My heart rate sped as he stared into my eyes, surely this fast of a heartbeat couldn't be healthy. "*Please?*" I couldn't remember if he was a hypnotist or not but he certainly seemed to get everything he wanted, especially when he was curious. He was *always* curious, but it wasn't a bad thing.

"Faelinin flowers." His eyes widened in surprise and shock.

"Really?" he asked, stunned. "I'd be lying if I said I wasn't surprised, Lorcan. That doesn't seem like something you'd be into." I had done a lot of questionable things today, half of them I likely would one hundred percent share with Balarin, no matter how much or how little I actually trusted him.

"It's for Bowen. Not to smoke," I said. Balarin raised his eyebrows sceptically.

"But you said—"

"I know what I said," I hissed, "but I don't want to kill a child or get high."

"No one does, Lorcan, except maybe the second one." He winked at me.

"Bowen does." Balarin tilted his head in acknowledgement before speaking again.

"He'd probably be down for both honestly." I ignored that.

"I don't know what to do!" I fretted. "I have to kill a child or suffer a death sentence from Bowen, but I want to kill him, not Caelan. They're a child. I'm scared of what Bowen will do if I disobey, and he's made it clear life in our family don't matter—" Balarin silenced my worry with his lips but not even his mouth and his distinct scent of coconut and vanilla with a hint of incense that told me he was close to me could solve everything forever, that they could for now and I'd accept any welcome distraction I could, especially from him.

"Better?" he asked. His eyes softened from love stricken to worried and concerned when I didn't answer.

"Oh, brave immortal Balarin of the Caves of Cummacdh and last Skin-Walker in the realm." His pupils turned to slits, quite literally. "Can you do something for me?"

"I *love* it when you use my full title." His eyes went back to normal, and their orange glow seemed almost softer than before. "I'll do anything for you, meu amor."

"Anything?"

"*Anything.*" His voice was almost a purr. "I would burn Faelan for you, Lorcan Isan."

"Good to know," I replied. "Would you die for me?" I asked, teasingly. Balarin froze, all previous confidence and charisma gone. Replaced by shock and worry about what his lover, I, had just proposed he do.

"Die?!" Balarin exclaimed, likely stunned by the implication of a world without his flair for drama. "For you?" He laughed nervously after the initial bout of shock. "What do you mean die? Don't get me wrong I love you but—" I put a finger to his lips. He looked at my black painted nails, up at my face, then to my lips and then back to my nails. He swallowed.

"Black suits you," he muttered, eyeing my nails again. "They need a trim, don't you think?" Attempting to diffuse the tension between us.

"Cale o fodido por favor, Balarin," I hissed. "Antes de facerte."

"Yes sir," he mumbled. The *clunk* of boots came from the hall and were getting progressively nearer to the door. I froze and stared at the shiny, brass doorknob. Balarin jumped up, but I didn't see where he went, only heard a drawer open and shut but I ignored it.

"Go," I hissed, gesturing to the window, still not looking away from the doorknob. Balarin bolted, wrenching open the window and looking back at me over his shoulder.

"We'll continue this conversation tomorrow," he said, leaping out the window and shifting halfway through and disappearing into the night. Just then there was a timid knock at the door.

"Yes?" I called, feigning a sleepy voice.

"Are you alright?" Caelan asked from the other side of the door.

"We thought we heard voices," Bowen hissed. *Dammit.*

"I'm alright," I assured them. "I was likely just talking in my sleep," I lied.

"I told you there was nothing!" Bowen yelled. "Keep your mouth shut and get back to bed you useless anaco de merda!" The sound of leather boots hitting flesh came from the opposite side of the door. I leapt out of bed and threw the door open seeing Caelan on the floor whimpering.

"What's going on?" I growled. Bowen came out from behind the door, a red mark blooming on his face.

"You hit me," Bowen growled back. "I'll hit you." I arched my wings above my head, asserting dominance over Bowen who was smaller than me.

"Please," Caelan murmured. "Stop fighting each other and go back to bed."

"Let me escort you back to your room, I'll teach you a lesson on eavesdropping," Bowen said, a bruise beginning to blossom on his cheek. Caelan whimpered again and began to stand up and limp back to their room. "I can help," Bowen insisted, grabbing his elbow and yanking Caelan down the hall.

"Take your hands off them," I snarled.

"*Fine*," he hissed, relinquishing his hold on Caelan's arm. The moment they were free, Caelan recoiled away, and I hurried over to them to offer support.

"Here," I whispered. "Lean on me." I wrapped my arm around Caelan's torso, bent down, and lifted them up into my arms and carried them to their room.

"Thank you," Caelan said quietly, as I lit a candle and placed it on their bedside table beside their glass of water upon which the condensation was already forming in the cold of the evening.

"Whatever for?" I asked, extinguishing the flame of the match and placing it in a small saucer. Caelan didn't make eye contact with me as I spoke to them as if with guilt. "Helping you?" Caelan fluffed their pillow and pulled their quilt over their shoulders, burrowing into the cotton fabric until only their red hair was visible. "It wasn't your fault."

"I know, but you didn't have to step in," Caelan mumbled. "I'm perfectly capable." I looked at them trying to see their face, but they weren't making eye contact with me. Whether it was on purpose or they hadn't noticed my questioning gaze, I couldn't tell and didn't want to continue the conversation if Caelan didn't wish to do so.

"I know, but you looked like you were struggling," I said, gently giving them a pat on the shoulder.

"I had it under control," they grumbled.

"Sure you did, kid," I chuckled. "Sleep well, Caelan."

~Balarin's Risk~

Two Years Ago

I stood outside in the silent, haunting courtyard looking out over the waves and the dark clouds rolling in, signalling the start of a gale. I watched the waves crash and pound against the cliff face, slowly eroding parts of the foundation upon which my family's legacy of abuse was founded. The sound of the sea calmed me and soothed my frayed nerves from Father's beating. The Caves of Cummacdh silhouetted against the bright red twin moons in the dark night gave the entire atmosphere a mood of suspense, and the air was thick and heavy with the smoke from the nymph's bonfires celebrating the moons annual alignment. I strolled around the grounds for a while. Listening to the screams coming from inside. Bowen had gone into his room after discipline, and I was the only one who wasn't otherwise incapacitated or being abused. The ciulama had not been properly prepared a few nights ago for supper. Luckily enough I was allergic to mushrooms and had to have something else that evening. Isan was considering starving me that evening but was in a rather decent mood due to a local robbery that he had been taking part in but hadn't been caught yet, and he was rather smug about this fact and proud of himself for it. That was until he got sick like everyone else and accused one of us spiking the dish, which we hadn't. That's also when he threw his little tantrum at being reduced to a mortal level and being prey to illness that us mere half breeds, that he had created mind you, were prone to. I spread my wings, letting the cold wind run through my feathers, and it felt amazing.

"Hello, Lorcan," a charming voice hissed. I turned around only to have Balarin wrap his arms around my waist and pull me closer to him. Almost holding me there beside him, I leaned into him, resting my head on his chest. He pressed his lips to the top of my head, and I felt an overwhelming feeling of belonging as he embraced me, and I could feel the beat of his steady heart through the fabric of his button-down.

"Hello, meu amor," I whispered, looking up at him, as his gentle smile turned to a smirk. Butterflies filled my hollow stomach, and I ensnared him in my wings. Pulling him closer to me so there was no space between us.

"Feeling lonely, are we?" Balarin chuckled, gently stroking my feathers. "This is where you come when you need serenity and re-assurance."

"I suppose you could say that," I responded in the most casual tone I could manage when I was around him. Balarin loosened his arms around me, and I pulled back my wings so we could see the moons above us easier.

"You know—" Balarin said, looking up at the glowing orbs in the sky and then back at me. "The glow of the moon compliments your attire." I looked at my clothes and then back up to look into his eyes set in his lovely face. I could stare at him for hours, if only we had that kind of time tonight.

"How so?" I asked.

"It looks as if your plumes are drenched in blood, it's...quite a nice look on you." I couldn't decide whether I should be intrigued by his words or to be afraid of them.

"Do you crave violence like Isan?" I asked. "Is that why the sight of blood appeals to you?" Balarin shook his head, chuckling to himself as if my question had an obvious answer.

"Blood rushes into your cheeks whenever you look at me," he whispered. Tracing patterns with his fingertip on my feathers, his eyes were otherwise occupied and lingered temporarily on my lips before focusing on his patterns again. A loud clap of thunder broke the intimate silence, and rain began to fall. Balarin grabbed my hand and pulled me under the leafy branches of a nearby tree, shielding me from the storm, his floor-length black coat swishing when he moved. My plumage was plastered to my skin and my hair, now wet from the sudden downpour was dripping onto my glasses. As I reached to remove them, Balarin stopped me. "Here." He chuckled. "Let me." He pulled a handkerchief from his left waistcoat pocket and took my glasses off my face, wiping them clean and then placing the handkerchief and my spectacles back into his pocket.

"I need those." I laughed. "Now I can't see." Even through the haze that was now my vision, I could see Balarin's eyes glowing, and I couldn't tell the emotion behind his eyes. Affection, attraction, perhaps something more. His eyes were soft, and my heart melted at the sight of him. He looked me up and down, his eyes focusing briefly on my lips and ending up settled on my collar.

"You look so handsome this evening," Balarin commented, stroking my cheek with the back of his hand, his touch sending a shock down my spine. His skin on my skin, caressing my cheek with his gentle fingertips as delicate as birds' wings and softer than a phoenix's feathers.

"May I confess something?" I asked. "And may I have your most sincere response?" He leaned down and looked me in the eyes, pupils dilating. The orange glow illuminating his face and complimenting his umber skin and dramatic eyeliner. His cheekbones, his concave nose, and his upturned eye-shape. Even his scent was a remarkable blend of vanilla and bergamot, hypnotising me like a manipulative spider luring the innocent tarantula hawk into his silky and beautiful web.

"You can tell me *anything*," Balarin whispered, his voice as smooth as velvet.

"Do you think it'll ever end?" I asked.

"However do you mean, Lorcan?" Balarin asked, arching an eyebrow. "Will what ever end, meu amor?"

"The legacy. The rules." I felt tears brimming in my eyes as I spoke. "Will I ever be able to not be scared of every decision that I make?" Balarin shrugged.

"What is life without a little rule breaking?" He smirked. His voice became seductive. "What is life without risks?" My breathing sped and his smile reached his eyes and it was…breathtaking. I fastened my fingers tightly around his collar and pulled his face lower and closer to mine, standing on my tiptoes, and I locked his lips with mine. His hands found their way to my waist, and he pulled me close so there was no distance between us. I was magnetised to him, I never wanted these feelings to end, I never wanted the moment to end. I desired that I could freeze time and forever live in this moment. But even to Skin-Walkers like Balarin, such things were impossible. The flames that had been merely embers until now were a blazing fire that filled my whole body. Balarin took one of his hands off my waist and rediscovered my face, tracing my jawline with one delicate finger, the band of his ring touching my skin. I tilted my face up so as to not hurt his neck when he kissed me. I released his lapel, and my hands found their way to his face. I pulled my mouth away from his. I looked up at him and saw that his eyes were full of light and affection. People had said for years that eyes are the windows to the soul, and as he watched me I felt as if I could see right through him. His soul was gorgeous, and I loved it as much as I loved the rest of him.

"I think I rather like being a rule breaker," I said. My breathing was definitely not as steady as it should be. I stroked his cheek with my thumb. Balarin smirked. "But if I ever say stop, and you don't there *will* be consequences," I hissed.

"Understood, sir." His voice took on a faint note of fear as he said this, hearing the seriousness of my tone.

"Lorcan!" I jumped, startled. Isan was yelling for me from inside, and I was scared as to how much he had seen.

"I'll see you soon, meu amor." Balarin brushed his lips against my cheek and disappeared in the downpour. I darted into the manor through the rain, but the weight of my drenched wings made this more difficult than it usually would've been. Isan wasn't fond of us not being punctual. It was going to be a long night, a long *painful* night.

~The Loss of the Lord~

Six Months Ago

The smell of roasting venison and chopped and sauteed doce peppers overwhelmed my senses and made my mouth water as Balarin and I strolled down the streets of Fogar. The smallest and most vital town on the island, known for its wares and many varieties of fresh produce imported from anywhere and everywhere across the island. We were the only people out and about this early, except for the vendors who would occasionally smile and wave at me, and I would awkwardly reciprocate their gestures. Balarin, on the other hand, was ignored by them, fear in their eyes as he passed.

"Are you alright, meu amor?" Balarin asked, unbothered by their obliviousness to him, gently nudging me with his shoulder to get my attention.

"Hmm?"

"You've been awfully quiet this afternoon," he stated. "Is there anything on your mind? You can tell me anything, you know," he added as an afterthought, cocking his head to the side, patiently awaiting my response. I shrugged.

"Caelan seemed on edge last night when I tucked them in. I'm just worried about them." I remembered them not meeting my gaze last night but whether it was intentionally or not, I couldn't tell.

"Teenagers." Balarin chuckled. "It's likely nothing, I wouldn't worry too much about it."

"Yeah," I laughed. "You're probably right." He took my hand and intertwined his fingers with mine as we walked. I held onto his arm and leaned into him, feeling the comfort of his presence which was almost too good to be true and honestly maybe was. Balarin leaned down and brushed his lips against the top of my head. I sighed, breathing in his scent.

"Hmm?" Balarin mumbled, looking up, and then I heard it. I ran, letting go of a stunned Balarin's arm before slowing to a halt at the edge of a small decline that led to the bottom of a ravine, I slid down the embankment and clambered over the rocks toward the river's edge, trying to find the source of the high-pitched scream. A small child was clinging onto a rock on the opposite side, flailing and struggling and trying to fight the current and hold on, their vividly red hair plastered to their scalp.

"Arghh!" I groaned, immediately recognizing the small, frail frame of the child in the river. Balarin stumbled down the small embankment after me, brushing his black hair out of his eyes before following my gaze and seeing the source of the racket.

"Dammit," he hissed. "And here I was hoping for an uneventful morning stroll through town." I looked over my shoulder at Balarin, as I unbuttoned my shirt.

"As was I." Balarin's eyes widened, and I couldn't quite tell what his expression was. Surprise or confusion? I couldn't tell.

"What are you doing?" he asked, horrified.

"What?" I asked with a smirk, guiding my wings through the slits in my shirt. "Never seen a lord in nothing but jeans?" I asked, teasingly. He shook his head, wordlessly.

"Not except you, this *really* takes me back," Balarin replied. I folded my wings to my back and dived into the river, swimming against the current and reaching the rock in about a minute. I wrapped my arm around Caelan's waist and led them through the water, which was a lot more difficult than I expected it would be, and pulled them out of the river and onto the bank. Caelan coughed and spluttered, getting the water out of their lungs.

"Your cloak, please, Balarin." Still temporarily mute, he unbuttoned the garment from around his neck and handed it to me. I took it from his hand and tenderly wrapped it around Caelan's frail shoulders and attempted to brush stray water droplets from their wings as I did so. "What the fuck are you doing out here this early in the morning?" I demanded to know, but Caelan was unconscious, likely due to the freezing water their system had gone into shock causing them to pass out. I rolled my eyes. "Balarin, please pick up my shirt and cloak. I'm going to carry Caelan to Elowyn's." Balarin nodded and scooped up my clothes, as I supported Caelan's head and neck in the crease of my elbow and lifted them up bridal style.

"You're still in your pants," Balarin whispered. "Aren't you going to put your top back on?"

"I don't believe there's time. I will later," I said, as I began walking away. Balarin hastily stuffed my clothing into his satchel before running after me and scrambling up the incline.

"Here." He tossed his bag down to me. "Mother would have a *lot* of questions if you showed up without a shirt on." It sounded like an excuse more than an actual reason to me.

"What?" I asked, as I opened the satchel. "Am I being distracting?"

"Perhaps just a little," Balarin replied, as I slung the strap of the bag over my shoulder. He extended his arm to me and hoisted me up over the edge. "I don't recall you being quite that muscular. That's all it is," he assured me. "I'm rather surprised."

"Are you sure that's all it is?" I asked. "Sure it's not anything else?" Balarin looked at me nervously.

"Absolutely."

"Whatever you say, meu amor." I scooped up Caelan in my arms and started walking.

"What do you think they were doing out here?" Balarin asked, recovering from his episode. "Isn't it quite early for a 12-year-old to be out on their own?" I nodded.

"My guess is they weren't alone." I saw the realisation in his eyes as he realised what I meant.

"You don't think…"

"I do," I replied. "It's a definite possibility that Bowen believed I wouldn't come through." If that was the case, I could be in danger. I didn't know where Bowen was on the island; he was an adult with free will to roam where he wished. If that was the case, no one in Faelan was safe.

"Should I alert the council?" Balarin inquired, his voice fraught with concern.

"That may be for the best." We'd reached our destination. "I'll get Caelan sorted and we can meet back at the manor once we've finished our respective tasks." Balarin nodded, brushing his lips against my cheek.

"Be safe," he whispered against my skin. "I don't want you getting hurt, you know how my mother is." And then he was gone. I lifted Caelan over my right shoulder, freeing my arm. I knocked twice and the door swung open. Elowyn's orange glowing eyes peered at me through the gloom, and she smiled a very toothy grin.

"What is it, Lorcan?" she asked, grudgingly. Finally someone who didn't use my title, someone who saw me as an equal but maybe she saw me as less.

"May I come in?" She stepped aside and strode in, a sign for me to follow, and I laid Caelan gently on the sofa, trying not to jostle their head too much.

"Oh gods!" she exclaimed. "What happened?" She placed a wrinkled hand on their forehead, checking their temperature. "They're freezing!" She turned to glower at me. "What did you do?"

"Nothing!" I protested, rustling my wings. "Your son and I found them this way. They were clinging to a rock in the river down by the ravine once they were out of the water they fainted."

"Hmm…" She considered this for a second. "What were you two doing there?" she asked, noting my half-buttoned shirt.

"No, it's not what you think," I assured her. Elowyn raised her eyebrows sceptically. "We weren't-we've-*I'd* never—"

"You didn't answer my question," she hissed.

"I took off my shirt so it wouldn't get wet, it's a sensory thing," I promised. "Can we just focus on Caelan?"

"Whatever you say, Lorcan," she said suspiciously. "Change the subject, why don't you." I rolled my eyes. "Escorio emplumada," she muttered under her breath as she made her way to the counter and started crushing herbs in a small dish and mixing the remnants with various odiferous liquids I had no name for.

"I heard that," I told her in the harshest voice I could manage. "Balarin *loves* my wings, I don't see why you're so upset."

"My son has dreadful taste, if that's the case," she said, pouring the foul-smelling concoction into a small bowl. "They're hideous, I swear, sometimes I think that boy is just around you for status." She dipped her fingers in the viridian-coloured liquid.

"I'm sure that's not true," I said, uneasily, and I watched as Elowyn gently smeared it on Caelan's forehead in a complex pattern composed of ancient runes.

"You don't know that," she muttered. "He's always been a good actor, Lorcan." Caelan's eyes snapped open and they sat bolt upright, shivering and looking around anxiously. Their icy blue eyes darted around the room, taking it all in at once. The dried herbs hanging from the ceiling, the overwhelming scent of something rotting, the weird crystals in the corner emitting steam, and a weird series of snaps and pops for no evident reason. There was something boiling in the cast iron pot over the sage green fire in the hearth across from the bed and the overwhelming heat was inescapable.

"Where am I?" they asked, their voice full of a command I had never heard escape their mouth. "I demand to know where I am." Their gaze turned to me, their eyes were slightly unfocused. "I know you," they said drunkenly, poking me in the chest.

"Yes, yes, you do," I said, taking their hand to stop their incessant poking. "Did Bowen do this?" I asked. Elowyn's eyes widened.

"Bowen did this!?" she exclaimed. "Why didn't you lead with that bastard!?"

"It's a theory." I sighed exasperatedly, ignoring her hurtful words and tone. There was a knock at the door. Elowyn stood up, but I beat her to it. "I'm on it," I told her. "Oh," I added, turning to look at her, "my parents were married." She rolled her eyes, and then I continued weaving around the various objects cluttering the floor until I finally made it to the door. I opened it and there was Balarin, his expression a mix of emotions. Worry, concern, befuddlement. I wrapped my arms around his waist pulling him close. He brushed his lips against my cheek.

"Are you alright?" he asked, looking me directly in the eyes with his hypnotic stare.

"Yes, just glad to see you again. Your mother is driving me absolutely tolo." Balarin chuckled.

"Try *living* with her for 21 years, it's a nightmare."

"I support you two, but you two shouldn't be doing things in public!" Elowyn yelled from inside. "I raised you better than that, Balarin. We used to be a respectable family when your father was alive." My face burned with embarrassment, and Balarin looked terrified.

"What were you telling her?" he asked, a note of horror in his voice.

"Your mother wanted to know why I was almost shirtless and took it the wrong way entirely. I didn't do anything." His eyes widened.

"Mother!" he yelled. And Elowyn's annoyingly loud raucous laugh filled the awkward silence between the three of us.

"You're just like your father, easily embarrassed, except he'd *never* be caught dead or alive with a faerie let alone a faerie of the same sex."

"What did the council say?" I asked, ignoring his mother, and hoping against hope he'd do the same. "Did they find him? Did they say anything?" Balarin's face fell.

"Err…about that," he began. "He didn't do it." I arched an eyebrow suspiciously.

"What do you mean?" I inquired. "Did he not confess?" He swallowed, and took a deep breath before speaking again, his face becoming a serious mask.

"His body was found by the delta."

~Broken Promises~

Present Day

"Did you figure out how Bowen died?" Balarin asked, looking up at me from the floor beside the throne, taking a sip from his flask and then passing it to me. I wiped tears from my cheek using the cuff of my shirt sleeve.

"Yesterday Boyd finished the autopsy. It was Faelinin, whether excessive smoking of it or direct ingestion of the flower, no one knows for sure." I took a sip of mead, feeling a lump rise in my throat, and then handed it back to Balarin who casually looked me up and down nervously as I spoke.

"Isn't that what you were going to use?" I nodded. "But you didn't—"

I cut him off. "No." Balarin contemplated this thoughtfully as he stroked my feathers. I leaned into his touch, craving an escape from my emotional distress. "And Caelan?" he began. "Any news?" My heart sank in my chest. Balarin gently placed his hand on mine. "Is it bad?" he asked, his voice taking on a more anxious and comforting tone.

"The funeral was yesterday," I replied. Balarin gently placed his hands under my shoulders and pulled me down from the throne onto his lap, wrapping his arms around me and pulling me close to his chest, and I could feel the rhythm of his beating heart through his shirt.

"If you don't mind me asking," Balarin began, "what happened?" He adjusted my circlet. "You don't really talk about it much…about the, erm, incident."

"Hypothermia. Our leading theory is that Bowen lured them out, thinking I wouldn't follow through, and took matters into his own hands." I sighed. No one would want a 12-year-old's blood on their hands and the possible societal backlash that would follow. Not even Bowen would be able to live through that. "We *think* he took a dose of Faelinin to end his life before we could do something worse and pulled Caelan into the river, knowing he'd die either way, whether Caelan went down with him or not," I continued.

"Pity," Balarin said, dismissively. "Caelan would have loved the Fallen Festival, they finally would've been able to attend, they would have loved it."

"We'll never know," I muttered. Being lord of Faelan after your two predecessors were eliminated within hours of each other meant that all eyes were on you, even if you were innocent. Nymphs luckily weren't the brightest species on the island and hadn't been able to connect the ever-so-obvious dots. They were more focused on the fact that the new Lord had a lover that was feared all over the island. Balarin may have been labelled as a Skin-Walker but he wasn't a pure one; his father on the other hand, was. He couldn't shift but he had magic seen in the form of manipulation and charisma.

"Caelan was so young," Balarin mused, "so much to live for. May have been a genetic dead end but could have married into a powerful family."

"If you think about it closely, so am I." Balarin looked down at me, arching an eyebrow.

"How so?" He chucked.

"I'm a homosexual," I replied, gently stroking his cheek as he had done to me so many times. "Surely you of all people know that by now." I laughed. He tilted my chin up so his gaze directly met mine, his piercing orange eyes staring into my soul, leaning down so I could hear him easier and clearer.

"That's not what I meant," he whispered seductively, his cool breath caressing my ear, all former anxiety gone. "I stated two things not one, meu amor." My heart raced as his hand found its way to my hip, and he pulled me closer to him. The red moonlight filtered in through the curtains of the throne room, giving the room an intimate glow that the two of us shared. He helped me to my feet before whipping around, grabbing my lapel, and slamming me against the tile while. "You're *mine*, Lord Oheria."

"Was that ever even a question?" I asked, feeling dizzy. "I thought we always knew that." A smirk crept across his face like ivy. Carefully, he removed my spectacles and gently tossed them onto the throne, and I heard a small thump when they landed on the padded cushion.

"You won't need these," he said, playfully. He pressed his lips to mine fervently, the scent of him overwhelming me, the taste of mead still on his lips. His fingers traced a line down my jaw, his other hand found its way to the back of my neck, and he pulled my face still impossibly closer to his. He wrapped his arms around my waist and listed me onto the throne so our faces were more level. Balarin broke away, meeting my gaze. "Am I a burden?" he asked. I shook my head.

"Never, Mr. Landry." I cupped his face with my hands. "You're the anchor to my ship in the storm. I would've gone mad six months ago if not for you."

"Silly boy." He chuckled. "You would have to live in the moment for me if I were not here to live in it with you." I pulled his face to mine again. We stayed like that for a while, in each other's arms, the only sound in the room was our synchronised breathing.

"If only we could be like this forever," I whispered, as Balarin delicately traced patterns in my feathers.

"Tempting," he muttered, "but you're a lord now, with things to attend to." I sighed, recognizing the wisdom in his words. "Unless... " Balarin paused thoughtfully. "Never mind." He kissed me again, heat blossoming where his mouth met the skin of my jaw, his lips travelling to the curve of my neck, my breathing hitched in the back of my throat, adrenaline caused by fear or feeling making comprehensible thought nearly impossible. His hands moved to the back of the throne, his arms acting as a cage of intimacy around me, the moonlight painted the floor red as if the tiles were covered in blood. This kiss was different from any other we had shared in this room or anywhere else; I wasn't positive how this made me feel. I had duties as Lord, things I *had* to do. Balarin was only a distraction from my responsibility, and it was time to put my Legacy first.

"Please stop," I muttered, my voice barely above a whisper. I placed my hands on his chest, pushing him away, but he didn't move. I forcefully shoved him away and he stumbled back. "I said, *stop*." I lowered my voice asserting dominance over Balarin. I got up, planting my feet firmly on the floor, arching my wings above my head making myself appear larger than I really was. "Do you not remember what I said?" I asked, my tone harsh and cold. Balarin cowered, scrambling away from me, and I was scared of who I was becoming, seeing my lover fearful in my presence but I didn't regret my course of action. I'd set my boundaries, and he had crossed them. I stepped down and walked toward him, feeling powerful and in control for the first time in my life. I just hadn't planned it this way.

"I'm sorry, I forgot, it won't happen again." He bowed his head, not meeting my gaze. I knelt down, ignoring the iciness of the tiles. I clamped my hand on his chin, tilting his face up, so he had no choice but look me in the eyes, and I could see the fear there. I drew my dagger, swiftly slicing a line across his wrist. Balarin yelped with pain, recoiling away from the blade.

"You broke your promise," I hissed.

"Are you mad?" he asked, tightly gripping his wound. "What the fuck, Lorcan!"

"You broke your promise," I repeated. "I told you I wouldn't take it lightly, that there'd be consequences if you didn't stop when I asked." I got up, turning and facing the window, the red light spilling in through the billowy curtains. "You're free to leave, Mr. Landry."

"See you at the Festival." I heard the doors open and close, and waited until I was sure he was gone. I sighed. Balarin was always manipulative, I just never thought he used it to get to me. Looking back, had he ever really cared? Or was it my status that mattered to him as he'd only started coming around more after I was in the throne. He hadn't been born with power, and he had used me to get it. I sighed again. I made the right choice. Bowen had been right all along after all. I hurried to my room, darting up the stairs, my boots clattering and echoing ominously as I went, my coat, a gift from Balarin, swished as I went around the corner and to my room. Grabbing a piece of paper and pen, I began to write feverishly, taking a sip from the flask that Balarin had left behind and I had stored in my pocket. I pushed my glasses up the bridge of my nose and took out another paper and continued to write. It was going to be a long night.

~The Fallen Festival~

The Next Day

A harsh rap on the door is what woke me, not the freezing cold or even the pounding ache in my head from the alcohol. I got up slowly, feeling dizzy as I stood up, stumbling to the door and swinging it open. Some part of me wished it would be Balarin at the door, coming back to me to apologise, but I should've known not to get my hopes up.

"You good, Lorcan?" Fergal asked, tenderly. "You smell of whiskey, what were you doing last night?" I stretched my wings and ran my hand through my hair.

"I'll be alright," I murmured, readjusting my circlet. "And never you mind what I was doing," I said, shaking my head, attempting to clear the fogginess in it. "I need something to focus on, anything you'd suggest?" Fergal shrugged.

"The Fallen Festival?" he proposed.

"Fuck," I whispered. "I forgot about that." Fergal gently placed his hand on my shoulder.

"Take your time, brother. You're in no rush to get to Fogar, relax. I do, however, believe that Melodian would rather enjoy seeing you there." He winked, a smile creeping across his face. "If you know what I mean," he added. My throat was thick, and I chuckled, but it sounded more like a rough cough.

51

"She'll be disappointed," I mused.

"How so?" Feral asked, cocking his head to the side. "Are you not going?" I surveyed him over the rims of glasses, attempting to see if he was serious or not about his inquiry.

"Oh, I'm still going," I replied. "She just isn't going to dance with me. She's another species; it would be rather improper." A look of confusion danced across Fergal's face.

"That never stopped you with Balarin," he pointed out.

"That was different," I replied harshly, my tone ending the conversation.

"I'll go, you need to get dressed in your day clothes." With that, Fergal pivoted on his heel and walked away down the hall going to wake up Anam and Boyd. I closed my door and strode to the wardrobe, withdrawing a simple beige turtleneck with khaki pants and a black jacket. No one cared what you wore even if you had high status. I put on my circlet, the only thing separating me from everyone else on the island and left the room, hurrying down the stairs and out the door racing down to the village.

"Melodian!" I yelled. The nymph turned, her blonde braid flipping over her shoulder when she turned. She waved and continued directing people as to where various lanterns and garlands went. "Is there any way I can help?" I asked.

"That depends, Lord Oheria."

"Lorcan," I corrected. She sighed.

"It's Lord Oheria now, you can't deny it." I didn't argue; it wasn't a fight I was willing to die in. She patted my shoulder smugly, taking my silence as a victory. "You *could* help arrange flowers with Edein and Zyphrey, if you'd like." She gestured to a small table littered with ribbons and flowers. "If you don't want to do that, you can supervise." I surveyed her over the rims of my glasses.

"How's this for supervision?" I asked, teasingly. Melodian blushed, a burning crimson spreading across her freckled cheeks.

"A little." I laughed softly to myself before joining the two elderly women at their table laden with delicately fragranced blossoms, noting the fact that Melodian was watching my every moment.

"Hello, Edein," I said, offering my hand to the first woman and shaking it carefully, worried if I was too rough her entire hand might come off. "Zyphrey." I repeated the same action.

"You must be the new Lord," Zyphrey croaked, a small smile on her wise face. "Lorcan Oheria, was it?"

"Yes, I am," I replied, not wanting to meet her gaze. "My father and brother passed recently."

"Oh, I'm so sorry to hear that, dear," Edein chimed in. "It must be *so* difficult taking care of Faelan by yourself?"

"Not really," I answered, "I have my other siblings and a, er, *consultant*. However, he recently resigned without so much as a few days' notice."

"How impolite," Zyphrey added.

"Indeed." I laughed, reflecting on Balarin's behaviour. "I'm surprised he was employed as long as he was."

"Might I ask what the young lad's name was?" Edein asked.

"Balarin Landry," I said, my voice breaking on his name. Edein and Zyphrey looked at each other, perplexed and deep in thought, while I anxiously arranged lilies and intricate patterns and tied them up with orange ribbon, while I waited for one of them to speak again.

"You mean Elowyn's boy?" Edein inquired.

"That's him," I replied. Zyphrey audibly gasped at this. "What is it?" I asked. "You seem shocked."

"I just never took Balarin to be the rude type," she replied, still in shock. "He always seemed like such a charming young man, but I never fully trusted him after Seraphim's disappearance."

"He had nothing to do with that," I assured her. Seraphim, Balarin's father, was there when Mother died, and I doubt Father had ever let that slide. We all sat in silence, as we arranged the flowers and snuggly wrapped them in ribbons. As the twin suns set, the lanterns Melodian had helped set up began to glow in the darkness, their sage green light cast an eerie glow in contrast with the red moonlight. The music started up and a slow waltz-like melody began and started gently bobbing my head to the rhythm. I watched as the nymphs and faeries of Faelan spun around one another, the ladies, and occasional gentlemen, flowing skirts swishing and the graceful movement of both partners creating an intricate shared movement. I stood there watching from the edge of the crowd, enjoying seeing the glee on their faces. I felt a soft tap on my shoulder and turned to see who it was.

"Care to dance, Lord Oheria?" Melodian asked, her hand extended, palm up, waiting for me to take it. I gently pushed her hand away.

"Not this time, Melodian." She sighed, her face full of disappointment, her previously cheeky smile, now a polite frown. "I see you as a friend," I added, attempting to spare her feelings. "Nothing more."

"I understand," she replied. "It was a try, though, right?" she asked, attempting to receive some form of affirmation from me.

"I'll admit, it must have taken some courage to approach me in the wild," I admitted. "Perhaps another time."

"Good enough." Her smile returned with the idea of a potential future interaction, and she walked away with a slight spring in her step, approaching her brother Tanyan and pulling him onto the dance floor. He stared desperately at me, as Melodian stepped on his foot and attempted to initiate a waltz. "*You're on your own, amigo,*" I mouthed, flashing him a smile. He sighed and went along with his little sister's charade. He'd have extremely sore feet by tomorrow, knowing her. I chuckled and continued watching the merriment of my people, my first Fallen Festival as lord and the twin moons reached their peak in the night sky, brightly illuminating all of Faelan in perfect alignment so you could only see one, and gasps of shock and glee came from the crowd as they watched the cosmic occurrence and the joy that they had survived another year. A cold hand touched my shoulder, not quite tap but not quite a firm grip.

"Melodian," I growled, "I already said *no*." A soft chuckle came from the stranger.

"You said no last night, not today," the voice hissed, the cool touch going from my shoulder to my collar bone, settling near the base of my throat, the other hand idly stroking and stroking my feathers and tracing intricate patterns upon my wings with their fingertips. I froze, my blood turning to ice in my veins, and my heart stopped. "May I have this dance, meu amor?"

~Blood-Stained Chains~

Present Day

Balarin grabbed my wrist and dragged me onto the dance floor, pulling me into a slow waltz, one hand on my lower back, the other firmly gasping mine, our fingers intertwined. I attempted to get out of his arms, but his hands were bars of steel.

"Let me go," I hissed.

"Not until you explain what happened last night," he replied, coldly, taking my hand and spinning me around and pulling my back to his arms before turning and dipping me, my feathers gently brushing against the leafy forest floor.

"You're a distraction from my responsibilities," I replied, reluctantly, a lump rising in my throat. "I didn't have those before." Balarin glowered at me, not accepting that as an answer. "You didn't stop," I said, my voice cracking. "I told you to stop, you promised if I ever told you to stop you would. You *didn't.*"

"You didn't have to leave me," he said. "It was one time, it won't happen again. We could marry," he suggested. "Start over, rule Faelan together as partners." He brushed his thumb along my bottom lip, sending chills down my spine and, for a moment, I thought he meant it, and I couldn't help but consider the prospect of us being official. A couple bound in wedlock, but I knew it wouldn't be for love, at least not for him. "Or at least," he paused for a moment, "that *could* have happened had you not demanded I leave last night."

"We both know you'd eliminate me somehow once you were in a position of power," I pointed out.

"How could you say that, meu amor?" he asked, his voice full of false hurt.

"You lost the right to call me that when you broke the rule." He tilted my face so his eyes were staring into mine, and they didn't have that lovely glow anymore that made me fall in the beginning, or maybe I was blinded, and it was never there at all, only wishful thinking.

"I was *always* there for you, and you're leaving me for *one* mistake?" he asked in disbelief. "After *everything* I've done for you."

"You've done nothing but lie!" I protested. "You've never done anything for me!" Balarin glowered.

"You don't think Bowen actually committed suicide, do you?" Balarin laughed. "After everything he had going for him? Honestly, Lorcan." Balarin shook his head, stunned. "How'd it take you this long? You're better than this."

"I know you said you'd help but I didn't think you'd actually be the one to do it!" I hissed in disbelief. "Hell, I didn't even think you were capable of such things!"

"You seemed like you had a lot on your plate," Balarin said, his tone nonchalant. "As for what happened to Caelan, it must have been pure coincidence. I was just as shocked as you, and I wasn't acting even though we *both* know how good I am at that." His orange eyes bored into mine with calculated emotion. "Would I ever lie to you?" He gently trailed his fingers down the length of throat, feeling the pulse under my skin race as he touched me.

"Yes," I replied. I felt as if I was suffocating under his gaze, as if I'd never be able to escape his stare. He traced his fingertips across my collarbone under the delicate fabric of my turtleneck. "That's why my trust for you can't be fixed with a few words of affirmation."

"We both know you're too sensitive to rule on your own," he said, subtly guiding the two of us away from the lit dance floor and closer to the forest's edge. I felt vulnerable. Not being able to get away, not being able to fight back against someone I had loved for so long. He was taller and stronger than me; if he decided to hurt me, I wouldn't be able to adequately protect myself, however, his tone of authority was alluring, if not seductive, whether that was his intention or not, and I could feel my former disdain toward him crumbling. "I could help with that, you know." His words, soft and seductive…and dangerous. So dangerous. I knew it was over the moment I felt ferns brush against me and Balarin's cool breath brushing my neck, caressing my ear. One hand finding my waist and the other locking into my hair. He spun me around, my back to him so I couldn't see him as a trail of gentle kisses went from my cheek to my lips and to my jaw as if he was determined to claim me as his with his lips and it scared me.

"No, you can't," I told him, my breath hitching in my throat, either from fear or unresolved longing I couldn't tell. "If something were to happen to me, you wouldn't get power either way." He ignored this.

"*Please?*" he whispered. His voice was alluring and almost tempting, more than I had ever heard escape his soft lips before. I felt as if I was melting into him, but I knew it wasn't good for me; he was toxic. If I let him have this then I would likely fall for his sweet lies and promises again, and I'd never be able to escape the invisible chains that bound me to him.

"*Please?*" he repeated, his voice dripping with desire as he awaited my answer.

"No," I said, firmly. "No more chances."

"*Please,*" he said again, his voice becoming desperate. "I can't live without you by my side, Lorcan." His mouth found my collarbone, and I gasped as his lips made contact with my skin. "Stay with me." The only sounds around us were that of gently rustling leaves, the slow rushing of the stream, and Balarin's soft kisses.

"Then die," I replied, firmly standing my ground. I couldn't bear another heartbreak, especially from him. "At the very least stay away from me. I'm done, Balarin."

"I wasn't asking." My blood ran cold and turned to ice in my veins. He turned me so we were face to face, and his eyes weren't beautiful anymore—perhaps they never were. But if they ever had been they weren't now; now they were frightening and full of hostility toward the one thing preventing him from coming into power. Me.

"I hope I misheard that," I said, as aggressively as I could manage, attempting to assert my dominance over him but he was unfazed. He grabbed my wrists and pushed me against a nearby tree, forcefully pressing his mouth to mine. My boot made hard contact with his chest, throwing him back. I drew my dagger, arching my wings above my head.

"Cut the theatrics, Lorcan," he panted, positioning himself awkwardly as he attempted to get up off the leaves of the forest floor, his teeth bared.

"*Don't touch me*," I growled. "I could end your life right here, right now if I wanted too." Balarin got up and brushed himself off, making sure the damp foliage wouldn't ruin his waistcoat.

"I know you, Lorcan. You wouldn't da—" I lunged, and it took a few seconds for Balarin to fully realise what was happening and leap out of the way but not quite fast enough, and my blade made contact with his arm, leaving a gash on the side of his face.

"Suppose you don't know me as well as you thought."

"You're mine, Oheria," he whispered. "Have you forgotten everything that we've done?" He reached toward my belt, his fingers nearing the buckle, and I pushed him away.

"How could I?" I asked. "You were perfect." I choked on tears and began sobbing, not realising my fatal mistake.

"I can be, just this time, without you." He dove, my blade he had taken from its sheath on my belt sinking into the flesh of my abdomen. I screamed, the cry ringing through the forest, and it seemed as if the trees themselves had recoiled from the harsh sound.

"Please, Balarin," I gasped. He didn't say anything. He twisted the serrated dagger, savouring my whimpers and screams of pain. I crumpled, the weapon still buried in my skin. My laboured breathing was the only sound I could hear anymore, there was no point in screaming.

"If I can't rule beside you, neither of us will." He shrugged. "Perhaps someday I'll take my chances with your brothers."

"Don't you fucking dare touch them," I hissed, mustering my last remaining strength, removing my blade and dragging myself toward him. "I'll find you beyond the grave, and I promise you, Omisha will have a special place in hell for you Balarin."

"I'm not scared of death," he responded. "I've cheated her before." He turned to leave, abandoning me and leaving me for dead. How was I surprised that this is how it would end? I should've known that my brother was right, and he was no good. That he was using me, but how could I? He had whispered me words of affirmation, but they were just sweet nothings to him and so much more to me, and I had a duty to my people in my final minutes. And that was making sure no one was hurt by him again. Ignoring my dizziness, the growing crimson stain upon my shirt and the pool of scarlet liquid upon the leaves I got up, feeling faint as if I were going to be sick, and I was surprised that I was still standing. I stumbled, but luckily he didn't hear it and kept going. I drew the dagger weakly and threw myself at him, and with my last amount of strength, stabbed him in the back. He fell forward, not knowing what was happening. I removed the blade and pierced him again and again and again until he was no longer breathing and his heart had stopped beating. Puncturing his cold heart, lungs, and trachea, each thrust of the blade being more fatal than the last, the worst part was that he hadn't made a single sound…not even a plea or a whisper for mercy as if he knew it was coming and knew that karma was out for him, putting on a brave face hoping he'd be right, but not this time. A quiet death he didn't deserve. Gasping and bleeding, I stared up at the stars, my breathing and heartbeat getting weaker and weaker all the while, and red moons shone through the haze of my rapidly-fading sight. A crimson moon, the colour of my blood and wounds, the crimson moons that symbolised the death of a king who had never been given the chance to reign, and I would forever be in hell for my sins…and now that it was over. I sighed, my final breath escaping my lungs and the stars vanished from sight.

The End

~Epilogue~

One Month Later

It was only a few hours after their deaths that their bodies were found. Balarin and Lorcan had collapsed in the forest, and we all couldn't help but wonder what had happened or why. They had both seemed so agreeable the weeks, months, and years prior to their demise but after going through Lorcan's belongings not only did we find a will, but a letter along with it.

To Whomever It May Concern,

When I pass, I wish no power of mine to go to Balarin, but to Melodian. She has supervised the festivals for years, and I've seen her commitment to her tasks in real time, she would be not only a good candidate but she would end the line of cruelty no one on the outside of my family has seen, and if all goes to plan, end the generations of trauma that have haunted the Oheria Legacy. With this in mind, my brothers shall still be allowed to live on the premises and should still be entitled to their share of the family fortune, do what you will with the rest. Please, take care of Faelan better than I, or my father ever could. I will forever be awaiting redemption for what I have done and what I hope to someday do, but at least do what you can, not for me—I don't deserve it—but for the people of Faelan.

Sincerely, Lorcan Oheria the Late Lord of Faelan

I was rather scared when I heard this, me, a ruler and a leader. It never seemed as Lorcan had ever liked me, but he had evidently seen something in me that I hadn't. I'd miss him but I'd make sure that his death wasn't in vain and prove to Faelan and to myself that I was worth this position and all the power it held. It didn't matter what Lorcan had done or what had happened between him and Balarin, the past was the past and the future was the future, and we had to move on stronger than before, and we would move forward stronger than before. A path forged in redemption in the name of Faelan itself.